☞ **W9-CKJ-358**

DAVID'S FATHER

DAVID'S FATHER

Story
by Robert N. Munsch

Art
Michael Martchenko

Annick Press Ltd.
Toronto • New York • Vancouver

Twenty-fourth printing, October 2005

Annick Press Ltd.

We acknowledge the support of the Canada Council for the Arts, the Ontario
Arts Council, and the Government of Canada through the Book Publishing
Industry Development Program (BPIDP) for our publishing activities.

Cataloging in Publication Data
    Munsch, Robert N., 1945-
      David's father

    (Munsch for kids)
    ISBN 0-920236-62-6 (bound) — ISBN 0-920236-64-2 (pbk.)

    I. Martchenko, Michael. II. Title. III. Series:
    Munsch, Robert N., 1945-   Munsch for kids

    PS8576.U58D39 1983   jC813'.54   C83-098820-3
    PZ7.M86Da 1983

Distributed in Canada by:
Firefly Books Ltd.
66 Leek Crescent
Richmond Hill, ON
L4B 1H1

Printed and bound in China.

Published in the U.S.A. by Annick Press (U.S.) Ltd.
Distributed in the U.S.A. by:
Firefly Books (U.S.) Inc.
P.O. Box 1338
Ellicott Station
Buffalo, NY 14205

visit us at: **www.annickpress.com**

To Julie

Julie was skipping home from school. She came to a large moving van. A man came out carrying a spoon—only it was as big as a shovel. Another man came out carrying a fork—only it was as big as a pitchfork. A third man came out carrying a knife—only it was as big as a flagpole.

"Yikes," said Julie, "I don't want to get to know these people at all."

She ran all the way home and hid under her bed till dinner time.

The next day Julie was skipping home from school again. A boy was standing where the moving van had been. He said, "Hi, my name's David. Would you like to come and play?" Julie looked at him very carefully. He seemed to be a regular sort of boy, so she stayed to play.

At five o'clock, from far away down the street, someone called, "Julie, come and eat."

"That's my mother," said Julie. Then someone called, **"DAVID!!!"**

"That's my father," said David.

Julie jumped up in the air, ran around in a circle three times, ran home and locked herself in her room till it was time for breakfast the next morning.

The next day Julie was skipping home and she saw David again. He said, "Hi, Julie, do you want to come and play?" Julie looked at him very, very carefully. He seemed to be a regular boy, so she stayed and played.

When it was almost five o'clock, David said, "Julie, please stay for dinner."

But Julie remembered the big knife, the big fork and the big spoon. "Well, I don't know," she said, "maybe it's a bad idea. I think maybe no. Good-bye, good-bye, good-bye."

"Well," said David, "we're having cheeseburgers, chocolate milk shakes and a salad."

"Oh?" said Julie, "I love cheeseburgers. I'll stay, I'll stay."

So they went into the kitchen. There was a small table with cheeseburgers, milk shakes and salads. On the other side of the room there was an enormous table. On it were a spoon as big as a shovel, a fork as big as a pitchfork and a knife as big as a flagpole. "David," whispered Julie, "who sits there?"

"Oh," said David. "That's where my father sits. You can hear him coming now." David's father sounded like this:

broum broum broum

He opened the door.

David's father was a giant. On his table there were 26 snails, three fried octopuses and 16 bricks covered with chocolate sauce.

David and Julie ate their cheeseburgers and the father ate the snails. David and Julie drank their milk shakes and the father ate the fried octopuses. David and Julie ate their salads and the father ate his chocolate-covered bricks.

David's father asked Julie if she would like a snail. Julie said no. David's father asked Julie if she would like an octopus. Julie said no. David's father asked Julie if she would like a delicious chocolate-covered brick. Julie said, "No, but please, may I have another milk shake?" So David's father made her another milk shake.

When they were done Julie said, very softly so the father couldn't hear, "David, you don't look very much like your father."

"Well, I'm adopted," said David.

"Oh," said Julie. "Well, do you like your father?"

"He's great," said David, "come for a walk and see."

So they walked down the street. Julie and David skipped, and the father went

broum broum broum.

They came to a road and they couldn't get across. The cars would not stop for David. The cars would not stop for Julie. The father walked into the middle of the road, looked at the cars and yelled,

"stop."

The cars all jumped up into the air, ran around in a circle three times and went back up the street so fast they forgot their tires.

Julie and David crossed the street and went into a store. The man who ran the store didn't like serving kids. They waited five minutes, 10 minutes, 15 minutes. Then David's father came in. He looked at the storekeeper and said, "THESE KIDS ARE MY FRIENDS!" The man jumped up into the air, ran around the store three times and gave David and Julie three boxes of ice cream, 11 bags of potato chips and 19 life savers, all for free. Julie and David walked down the street and went around a bend.

There were six big kids from grade eight standing in the middle of the sidewalk. They looked at David. They looked at Julie and they looked at the food. Then one big kid reached down and grabbed a box of ice cream. David's father came round the bend. He looked at the big kids and yelled,

"beat it."

They jumped right out of their shirts. They jumped right out of their pants and ran down the street in their underwear. Julie ran after them, but she slipped and scraped her elbow.

David's father picked her up and held her. Then he put a special giant bandage on her elbow.

Julie said, "Well, David, you do have a very nice father after all, but he is still kind of scary."

"You think he is scary?" said David. "Wait till you meet my grandmother."

Other books in the Munsch for Kids series: